W9-BIA-416

For Zöe and Clio

Copyright © 1992 by Sandy Nightingale
First published in Great Britain in 1992 by Andersen Press Ltd.
First United States edition 1992

All rights reserved. No part of this publication
may be reproduced or transmitted in any form or by any means,
electronic or mechanical, including photocopy, recording,
or any information storage and retrieval system,
without permission in writing from the publisher.

Requests for permission to make copies
of any part of the work should be mailed to: Permissions Department,
Harcourt Brace Jovanovich, Publishers, 8th Floor,
Orlando, Florida 32887.

Library of Congress Cataloging-in-Publication Data
Nightingale, Sandy.
Pink pigs aplenty/written and illustrated by Sandy Nightingale.
p.   cm.
Summary: Just how many pink pigs are there in the piggies circus
and what are those pastel porcine performers doing?
ISBN 0-15-261882-1
[1. Pigs — Fiction. 2. Circus — Fiction. 3. Counting.] I. Title.
PZ7.N583Pi   1992
[E] — dc20   91-45837

Printed in Italy

A B C D E

Pink Pigs Aplenty

SANDY NIGHTINGALE

HARCOURT BRACE JOVANOVICH, PUBLISHERS

SAN DIEGO   NEW YORK   LONDON

How many pink pigs are there in the piggies circus?

One pink pig
peeling potatoes.

Two pink pigs
painting pictures.

Three pink pigs
practicing pirouettes.

Four pink pigs
on a prancing
pantomime pony.

Five pink pigs
playing pirates.

Six pink pigs
on pogo sticks.

Seven pink pigs
throwing pies at a
picnic party.

Eight pink pigs
piloting planes.

Nine pink pigs
pillow fighting in
their pajamas.

Ten pink pigs
performing a piggy
pyramid.

Oops!

Perhaps they need more practice.